THE EMERALD BEAR

Ken Orchard

Illustrated by Jenny Kilgore

Providence House Publishers
WWW.PROVIDENCEHOUSE.COM
FRANKLIN, TENNESSEE

Printed in the United States of America

12   11   10   09   08   1   2   3   4   5

Library of Congress Control Number: 2008920242

ISBN: 978-1-57736-406-1

Illustrations by Jenny Kilgore
Cover and page design by LeAnna Massingille

PROVIDENCE HOUSE PUBLISHERS
238 Seaboard Lane • Franklin, Tennessee 37067
www.providencehouse.com
800-321-5692

To Jamie—with whom it all began
and
To Sidney—who liked the story

THE EMERALD BEAR

CHAPTER ONE

The family car moved slowly as it turned onto Willow Brook Lane, a narrow street lined with trees that had thick trunks and high branches. The houses on either side had broad front lawns, some with flower gardens under their front windows or along their sides.

It was a beautiful summer day, and the sun shone brightly as Sarah and her family drove up the block. With her face pressed against the window glass, Sarah could see the blue siding and large front windows of her new home.

The front yard had plenty of grass for playing and trees for shade, one of which had a swing hanging down from its great branches.

It doesn't look so bad, she thought.

Her brother, Benjamin, with his ever-present baseball cap pushed sideways on his head, peered out the other window of the car.

"Wow," he called to his father from the backseat. "There's even a basketball hoop on the garage!"

Benjamin was nine, a full two years older and almost a head taller than Sarah. As big brothers go, he was very special. He always looked out for Sarah, walking with her to school, helping her across streets, loaning her his books to read, and even letting her take turns at his favorite game—basketball.

Sarah and her family were moving to the new house because Mr. Williams had taken a new job nearby. They'd bought the house from another family who had moved out of the city.

Sarah noticed someone walking toward them so quickly that he was practically bouncing. "There's Mr. Bumble," Sarah's mother said as they pulled into the driveway.

"Hello, Mr. and Mrs. Williams! Welcome! Welcome to your new house!" Mr. Bumble called, waving his hand.

Mr. Bumble was the salesman who'd sold the house to Sarah's family. He was a short and chubby man, with red cheeks and eyeglasses that perched at the end of his nose. It made Sarah giggle to see him bounce about.

"Hello, Mr. Bumble," Mr. Williams said, as they all got out of the car. "How are you today?"

"Fine. Fine. Just fine, thank you," Mr. Bumble replied. "And I have the keys right here! Yes, indeedy! I have the keys to your new house right here!"

Mr. Bumble handed the keys to Mr. Williams. "Well, must go! Must go!" he said. "Lots of houses to sell today! Lots of houses, yes indeedy!"

He bounced down the street, waving as he went.

"What a funny little man," Sarah giggled.

"Wow, I'll say!" Benjamin agreed, laughing.

Mr. and Mrs. Williams smiled at their two children. "Do you want to go inside and look around?" Mr. Williams asked.

"Yes! Oh, yes!" Sarah and Benjamin shouted, as they ran up the walkway to the door.

"Hey! Wait for us!" Mrs. Williams laughed. "We have the keys!"

As the door swung open, Sarah's eyes opened wide at the sight of the big living room inside. On one wall was a huge fireplace, and in front of her, a large staircase led upstairs. Since only a small portion of the family's furniture had been delivered by the movers, the house looked even bigger.

"Why don't you two go up and look at your bedrooms?" Mr. Williams said.

As the children started up the wide stairs, Mrs. Williams called, "Don't forget. Your friends are coming by to help us unpack."

Benjamin and Sarah smiled at each other. Knowing their friends were coming would make moving into a strange new house more like fun.

Annie and Matt would be coming. So would the twins, Josh and Jeremy. Even Rachael was coming from far across town.

Of course, their friends' parents would be there, too, and Mrs. Williams was planning to make plenty of sandwiches for everyone while they worked and unpacked.

There would also be big jugs of iced tea to drink, and Rachael's mother was going to bring freshly baked oatmeal cookies for the occasion. Sarah's mouth watered at the thought of all that food.

Sarah and Benjamin found their new rooms at the top of the stairs. They were cozy rooms, with big windows that let in lots of sunlight. The movers had already placed several boxes marked "Children's Room" on the floor. Benjamin busied himself opening up a box in his room, hoping to find his prized rock collection.

Sarah wandered over to the big closet in her room and peeked inside. She saw there was room for clothes and for toys and for all sorts of things.

Sarah noticed some boxes piled in the corner. They didn't have any of the bright yellow moving tags like the one on the box Benjamin was opening.

She wondered if the people who lived there before had forgotten them.

Sarah squinted her eyes in the dim light of the closet, as she tried to make out what was there.

"Benjamin! Will you come down and help me, please?" Mrs. Williams called from downstairs.

"Coming!" Her brother hurried out his bedroom door.

Sarah turned to follow her brother when suddenly she saw something out of the corner of her eye.

She moved closer to get a better look. Something was back there among all those boxes.

She pushed the bigger boxes aside, and what she saw made her gasp with delight.

It was a little stuffed bear!

The bear's foot was stuck in a heating vent in the closet floor.

"You poor thing!" she said, as she bent down and gently pried the foot out of the vent. Then she carried the little fellow out of the closet and into the light of the bedroom.

"Why—you're green!"

She grinned and held him up with both arms to get a better look at him.

Sure enough! His fur was green, from the tips of his ears to the ends of his toes. He had dark brown eyes, a dark brown nose, and a sad smile that made Sarah think he had been in the closet for a long, long time.

Around his waist was a pair of chocolate brown pants with a golden stripe on the side; it looked a little like a soldier's uniform.

He was all covered with scuffs and lint, so Sarah set about cleaning up her new friend.

"What should I call you?" she said, as she brushed the lint from the top of his head. "You're a very strange-looking bear."

Sarah cleaned and brushed and brushed and cleaned. She was nearly finished when she heard a voice behind her.

"Whatcha got there, sweetheart?"

Sarah looked around and saw her father smiling down at her.

"Look what I found, Daddy," she said. "Isn't he wonderful?"

"Well, he's certainly an odd-looking fellow," Mr. Williams said, "And that color—emerald green! That's the color of kings and princes," he added.

"He must've been somebody very special once."

Sarah smiled and thought, *Yes, you're somebody special, all right. You're my very own new friend. My very own Emerald Bear.*

She hugged and kissed the bear and finished brushing the last of the lint from the bottom of his brown pants.

"There!" she said. "Almost as good as new!"

"Sarah! Sarah! They're here! They're here!" Benjamin called from the bottom of the stairs.

"It looks like your friends have arrived," Mr. Williams said. "Are you coming?"

Sarah sat the Emerald Bear on top of the boxes in the middle of her room and followed her father downstairs.

Benjamin, Matt, and the twins were already playing basketball by the garage, and Annie and Rachael were peeking up the chimney of the fireplace in the new living room, when Sarah joined them.

"Wow! What a great place!" Annie said. "I can't wait to come here for a long visit."

Sarah gave her friends a hug. "Wanna see the back-yard?" she asked.

The three girls spent the next few hours exploring the yard, helping with the unpacking, and playing around the big trees outside.

Soon it was time to eat, and the seven friends hurried inside with hungry appetites. There, Mrs. Williams and the other mothers were setting dishes around the table.

"Why don't you show your friends your room while I set out the sandwiches?" Mrs. Williams said.

"Yeah," said Rachael. "I want to see it. Does it have a fireplace, too?"

Sarah led the way up the stairs, with Rachael and the rest of her friends close behind.

Rachael was so anxious to see the new bedroom that she ran ahead of Sarah and through the door.

When Sarah entered the room, she saw Rachael standing by the boxes in the middle of the floor. Rachael had a funny look on her face.

"What's that?" Rachael laughed, pointing at the Emerald Bear. "A green bear! How silly!"

Rachael laughed and laughed. She laughed until her sides hurt! Matt and the twins laughed, too. Even Annie was laughing.

"What a funny-looking bear," Matt said.

"Yeah," Josh and Jeremy chuckled. "He's so green he should've been a frog, not a bear!"

Benjamin felt sorry for Sarah. He nudged the twins to make them stop laughing. Then he looked over at Sarah to see if he could help, but she was looking at the Emerald Bear's face. It looked so much sadder than before.

"You leave him alone!" Sarah said, with tears in her eyes.

She grabbed the Emerald Bear and ran from the room.

"Wait, Sarah!" Benjamin said, running after her.

Sarah raced back down the stairs with Benjamin right behind her. She ran directly into her father, who bent down and scooped her up into his arms.

"Whoa, there! Where are you going in such a hurry?" he said.

"Oh, Daddy," Sarah cried, "they were making fun of the Emerald Bear. They were being so mean. Make them stop, Daddy, make them stop!"

Sarah held the Emerald Bear close to her face and hid her tears in his soft, furry body.

Mr. Williams and Benjamin talked to Sarah and tried very hard to make her feel better, but all she could hear was the laughter coming from the top of the stairs.

Then, suddenly, the laughter stopped. It became very quiet in the room above. In fact, there wasn't a sound to be heard.

Benjamin looked at Mr. Williams and wrinkled his forehead. Mr. Williams stared at the door at the top of the stairs.

"Children?" he called. There was no answer.

Mr. Williams put Sarah down, and he and Benjamin climbed the stairs to her bedroom. When they entered the room, they couldn't believe their eyes. It was completely empty.

The boxes were still in the middle of the floor, but there were no children.

Mr. Williams peered into the closet. No children!

He walked over by the windows and around the room. No children!

He and Benjamin walked up and down the hallways and looked into all the upstairs rooms. No children!

Mr. Williams called to the other parents. Together they looked all over the house and all over the yard outside. They looked in every possible place they could think.

But no children!

It was getting late. Annie's mother looked worried. Matt's mother started to cry. All the parents were very concerned and upset.

Mr. Williams picked up the telephone and said, "We'd better call Sheriff Parker."

A few minutes after getting the phone call, the sheriff arrived in his police car, its blue lights flashing.

He was very kind and did his best to comfort all the parents.

"Don't worry," he said. "We'll find them." The sheriff pulled a small radio from a pouch on his belt and spoke into it, alerting his deputies about the missing children, and ensuring that all available officers would be looking for them.

The flashing police car lights had roused curious neighbors who, when they learned about what had happened, quickly volunteered to help search.

While Sheriff Parker and the fathers talked about how to proceed with the search, Mrs. Williams made coffee. It was going to be a long night.

Sarah and Benjamin looked at each other. They wondered where their friends could be.

Sarah held the Emerald Bear close. She looked at his face and the expression she saw on it made her feel as if he had a secret to tell.

"It's time you two got some sleep," Mrs. Williams said. "There's nothing you can do tonight anyway."

She led them up the stairs to Benjamin's room. Since the beds had not yet been assembled, Mrs. Williams spread two sleeping bags on the floor of the bedroom.

"I think it's best if you two stay together tonight," she said.

Then she plugged a small night-light into the socket by the door and placed a flashlight on the floor beside Benjamin.

Mrs. Williams tucked her children into their sleeping bags and kissed each one on the forehead.

"The glow from this night-light will help keep the darkness away," she said.

"Don't worry, Mommy," Sarah said. "I have Emerald Bear to protect us."

Mrs. Williams smiled and placed the Emerald Bear at the foot of Sarah's sleeping bag.

"Then I hope he guards you well tonight," she said. "Remember, we'll be just outside the door."

Mrs. Williams paused at the doorway. "Good night, my precious darlings," she added. Then she quietly closed the door.

Sarah looked at Benjamin. "Do you think something bad happened to Rachael and the others?" she asked.

"I don't know," Benjamin said sleepily. "Things will be better in the morning."

Sarah closed her eyes and tried to think. She thought about all that had happened this day. She wondered where her friends were.

Sleep slowly overcame her, and as it did, she could almost see Rachael's face and hear her voice.

CHAPTER TWO

"Sarah! Sarah!" a small voice said.

Oh, Rachael, Sarah thought. *Where are you, anyway?*

"Sarah! Sarah!" the small voice said again.

Wait a minute, Sarah thought. *That voice isn't in my dreams. It's in this room!*

"Sarah! Get up! Get up, Sarah. We must hurry!" the little voice said more urgently.

Sarah opened her eyes. "Who said that? Who's here?" She looked around, but all she saw was Benjamin sleeping and her bear beside her feet. She stared at him in disbelief.

The Emerald Bear was looking right at her. Suddenly, his mouth began to move.

"Hurry, Sarah. There's not much time."

"You can talk!" Sarah gasped.

"Of course I can, silly," laughed the Emerald Bear, and he stood up!

"But . . . but . . . how . . ." Sarah stammered.

"No time to explain now," the bear said. "We have to hurry if we're to save the children!"

"You know what happened to Rachael and the rest of my friends?" Sarah asked.

"Yes," the bear answered. "They've been taken by the Gruffs, through one of the secret doors of Ursanor!"

"Gruffs? Ursanor? What are you talking about?" Sarah asked.

"Ursanor is my home. It is also the home of the Gruffs and many others. It is through the secret doors that we travel to the Outside World of Children," the bear explained hurriedly. He grabbed her arm and tugged. "No more time for talk. We must go!"

"You have to tell this to Mommy and Daddy," Sarah said.

"No, Sarah," the Emerald Bear said, still holding her arm. "I can't talk to grown-ups. They don't understand. I can only talk to children in the Outside World. Only they are able to understand."

Benjamin began to stir. "Who are you talking to?" he mumbled.

"Wake up, Benjamin!" Sarah said, poking at her brother. "We're going to Ursanor!"

"Where?" Benjamin said in a sleepy voice.

"Let's go!" said the Emerald Bear, picking up the flashlight lying next to Benjamin's sleeping bag and leading the way toward Sarah's room.

Sarah held on tightly to the bear's hand.

Benjamin rubbed his eyes as he staggered after them. "You can talk!" he said to the bear.

"Of course he can, silly," Sarah laughed.

The bear led them into the darkened closet in Sarah's room and over to the boxes lying in the corner. Several of the boxes had been moved aside, revealing the edge of a small door.

"Yes, they came this way, all right," the Emerald Bear said.

He handed the flashlight to Benjamin, and then pushed aside the rest of the boxes.

By the light's beam, the children could see a door, not much bigger than the bear and barely large enough for Sarah and Benjamin to squeeze through. The wood of the door was painted the same bright color as the bear's fur.

The Emerald Bear pushed open the door and led the children into a long, dark tunnel.

Benjamin bent over to get through the little door. Once he was inside, he could stand up, and the three of them held hands as the flashlight guided them along the passageway.

At the far end of the tunnel, they saw a bright light.

"Where does this go?" asked Benjamin.

"To the Windy Woods at the far edge of Ursanor," answered the bear. "Only there can be found the secret tunnels and doors to the Outside World of Children."

He seemed to know his way well and hurried them along. As they drew near to the end of the tunnel, the light grew ever brighter.

"Don't be afraid, Sarah," the Emerald Bear said with a smile. "You're with me now."

Sarah smiled back. She wasn't scared at all, for she knew she was with a very special bear.

Soon, they stepped out of the tunnel and into a sunlit forest, with a blue sky above. The trees were taller and greener than any Sarah and Benjamin had seen before. There were flowers of many different colors and golden-colored grass everywhere.

The children heard the wind rushing through the leaves of the big trees. It was a strong wind.

Benjamin switched off the flashlight and turned back toward the tunnel, but there was no entrance to be seen. He only saw the trees of the forest spread out in all directions.

The bear led the children through the golden grass to a path that led through the Windy Woods and under the canopy of its great trees.

"This place is so beautiful," Sarah said. "Annie and Rachael and the others must be having lots of fun."

"Oh, no, Sarah," the Emerald Bear said. "They are in great danger. They were *taken*. They were taken by the Gruffs!"

Benjamin and Sarah looked at each other. "Who are the Gruffs?" her brother asked.

"The Gruffs live in a village by the Dark River," the bear explained. "It is far to the east in Ursanor. They've stolen your friends to lock up as prisoners."

"But why?" Sarah asked.

"Because they need children to show them how to have fun," the Emerald Bear said.

"For years the Gruffs have lived by themselves, without any friends. They've grown fearful of others and others have grown fearful of them. They're an unhappy people, without laughter, without joy, and gruff with everyone they meet.

"Then they heard about the Legend of the secret tunnels to the Outside World of Children and how the Emerald Bears travel there, and about the fun and the laughter of the children there," the bear continued. "They wanted these things for themselves.

"The Gruffs don't know any games, or any songs, or any rhymes, or any stories, or any of the fun things children know. So they took Rachael and your friends and will lock them up until they've taken those things from them."

"But that's terrible and mean," Sarah said.

"Yes," the bear replied. "The Gruffs have been mean for a very long time."

"But what can we do?" Benjamin asked. "There are only three of us."

"I know where we can find help," the Emerald Bear replied. "We'll go to the great castle of the Emerald Bears!"

The three had gone a long way along the path by now, and Benjamin and Sarah saw that they were coming to the edge of the woods. There, the path joined a narrow road.

The wind had stopped blowing and they saw that the road ahead split in three directions.

"That is the way to the Dark River and the Gruffs," said the bear, pointing straight ahead. Then he motioned to the road on the left. "We must go this way first, to find help."

He led the children down the road, which went over several hills, crossed many little streams, and trailed past fields of brightly colored flowers.

Then they came to a field full of flowers of only one color—emerald green. Among the green petals of the flowers were golden stems and golden leaves.

"We are very near now. These are the King's favorite flowers," said the Emerald Bear, laughing.

For the first time, Sarah saw that her bear was happy. But it was a longing kind of happiness.

"It's good to be home again," he said.

"Does a king live in the castle?" Benjamin asked.

"Oh, yes," said the bear very seriously. "King Wuzzlefuzz is the King of all Ursanor and the leader of the Emerald Bear Army. I'm sure he'll give us all the help we need. He's a very great King!"

The Emerald Bear took the children's hands and led them through the field of royal flowers and to the top of a small hill.

As they reached the top, the children's eyes grew wide with wonder, for before them was a magnificent castle with golden towers and wide stone walls.

Green banners flew from the tops of the towers and a great wooden drawbridge and doors stood at the center of the main castle wall. It was the most fantastic place Sarah had ever seen.

The bear looked up at the children and smiled. "Come on! Come on!" he said, running ahead. "No time to waste."

In a few steps, the three stood before the huge wooden doors of the castle. The Emerald Bear walked up to a large metal door knocker and knocked four times on the doors.

"Who goes there?" a voice from within said.

"A friend!" replied the bear.

Slowly, the great doors swung open and out stepped four small bears in soldier's uniforms.

Sarah and Benjamin looked at each other. Each one was the same color as the Emerald Bear, and each wore chocolate brown trousers with golden stripes on each side.

But these bears had matching coats, and on their heads were soldier's hats that had plumes on top.

One seemed very much in charge of the others, and Benjamin and Sarah could see sergeant stripes on the sleeve of his uniform.

"Sergeant Willow! Hello! How are you?" the Emerald Bear said with glee. "Don't you remember me? Has it been that long?"

A look of surprise came over Sergeant Willow's face. "Captain!" he exclaimed. "Can it really be you?"

He opened his arms to hug the Emerald Bear, but suddenly, he stopped short and snapped to attention.

"Arrest him!" Sergeant Willow yelled to the other bear guards.

"What?" the Emerald Bear exclaimed. "What's going on here?"

Benjamin and Sarah also could not believe what was happening.

"Sorry, sir," Sergeant Willow said sadly. "Orders are orders. The King left word that you were to be arrested on sight in Ursanor, along with anyone who accompanied you. I'm only doing my duty, sir. I'm afraid your friends are under arrest, too."

Before the children could do anything, the bear guards had drawn their swords and were leading them all inside the castle.

They led them into a wide courtyard that was just inside the gates, across an open space within, and to a small door on the far side of the courtyard.

Sarah was becoming frightened. "Where are you taking us?" she asked with a quiver.

"To the dungeon, I'm afraid," replied Sergeant Willow regretfully.

The bear sergeant led the group down a long, winding stairway. At the bottom of the stairs sat a rather tubby little bear behind a very official-looking desk.

He wore an officer's coat, with golden braid on the sleeves. He had puffy cheeks and a round little nose with a pair of spectacles perched on the end. Sarah thought he looked somewhat familiar.

Sergeant Willow stopped in front of the desk, saluted, and said, "Lieutenant Pitterpatter, I have three prisoners for the dungeon."

The tubby little bear looked up at the children and then over at the Emerald Bear. Then he jumped up to attention.

"Captain!" he said. "So good to see you again, sir. Yes, sir. Yes, indeedy. So good to see you again."

"No, no!" said Sergeant Willow. "The Captain is one of the prisoners."

"Oh, dear me, dear me," said Lieutenant Pitterpatter. "This is terrible, yes, indeedy, *terrible*. The Captain is a prisoner by the King's orders.

"But orders are orders, yes, indeedy, orders are orders," he continued sadly. "I must report this to the King at once! Put the prisoners in the dungeon!"

So the guards put the children, who were quite tired and a little scared after all that had happened, into the dungeon along with the Emerald Bear. Then they locked the door.

Sergeant Willow left one guard outside the door and then followed Lieutenant Pitterpatter up the stairs to report to the King.

Sarah could hear the bears talking as they hurried up the stairs. "Must hurry! Must hurry! No time to waste. The King is waiting!" Lieutenant Pitterpatter said.

That bear reminds me of someone, Sarah thought, but she couldn't remember who.

"This is a fine mess we're in," Benjamin said to the Emerald Bear.

Sarah began to cry. "I thought you said he was a great King and he would help us."

The Emerald Bear sat down beside Sarah and held her hands in his soft paws.

"Don't cry, Sarah," he said softly. "He really is a very good and wise King. I don't know what's happened here, but I'm sure everything will be all right. You'll see!"

But all Sarah and Benjamin could see were the dark, cold walls of the dungeon all around them.

CHAPTER THREE

Lieutenant Pitterpatter and Sergeant Willow hurried to the great throne room deep within the castle. The room was full of many different folk from all over Ursanor who had come to King Wuzzlefuzz's court.

In the middle of all the hustle and bustle sat the King himself, finely dressed in a chocolate brown uniform. He had many golden medals on his chest, an emerald green sash around his waist, and a golden crown on his head.

Lieutenant Pitterpatter and Sergeant Willow made straight for the foot of the throne and stood there at attention.

"Sire, we have the prisoners locked away in the dungeon, yes, indeedy, all locked away!" Lieutenant Pitterpatter said.

King Wuzzlefuzz was the largest of the Emerald Bears, with kind brown eyes and a brown beard on his chin. He spoke slowly and with a soft voice.

"What prisoners, Lieutenant?" the King asked.

"Why, the deserter, Sire, the Captain," replied Lieutenant Pitterpatter.

The King's eyes grew wide. "What!" he said. "You have captured . . . him!"

"Well, not exactly captured, Sire," Sergeant Willow said. "He sorta walked into the castle on his own."

"So," the King said. "He probably wants me to forgive him. But that trick won't work. The dungeon is too good for that deserter. And after all I've done for him, even making him Captain of the Bear Guard."

"Don't forget to tell him about the children," whispered Sergeant Willow to Lieutenant Pitterpatter.

"Children! What children?" bellowed King Wuzzlefuzz.

"Oh, yes, I almost forgot," Lieutenant Pitterpatter said.

"We also locked up two children who were with the deserter. Friends of his, no doubt," he added, very pleased with himself.

"Children! Children from the Outside World here in Ursanor!" bellowed the King again. "Release them at once and bring them to me!" he said, jumping to his feet. "The very idea, locking *children* up in my dungeon! Unheard of!"

Lieutenant Pitterpatter and Sergeant Willow hurried off and hastily returned with Sarah, Benjamin, and the former Captain of the Bear Guard.

The children were thankful to be rid of the dark and dreary dungeon and stood in wonder at the splendor of the throne room and the finery of all those attending the King's court.

King Wuzzlefuzz spoke softly and kindly as he approached the children.

"Welcome! Welcome, dear children! Welcome to the castle of the Emerald Bears!" he said. "I'm truly sorry for our inexcusable manners, but we don't get many children from the Outside World as visitors. In fact, you're the first!"

Sarah smiled back at the King of the Emerald Bears as she saw the kindness in his eyes. *Perhaps he is a good and wise King after all*, she thought.

"Thank you, Sir," Sarah said. "You have the most beautiful house I've ever seen!"

The King laughed heartily. "Why, thank you, child," he said. "Please think of my castle as your own home, and whatever my kingdom has to offer is yours for the asking."

Sarah gave the King a wide grin. "My name is Sarah, Sir, and this is my brother, Benjamin."

"And a fine-looking chap he is, too," the King said with another laugh.

"Is that a real crown?" Benjamin asked, pushing his own baseball cap back on his head.

The King began to laugh again, but stopped short when he saw the Captain, who was standing behind Benjamin. His look became quite stern, but Sarah glimpsed a little twinkle of gladness in the King's eyes.

"Well, Captain, it certainly has been a long time since you've been in this castle," the King said. "I hope you found our dungeon to your liking, because you're going to be spending a long time in it!"

"No! No! You can't!" Sarah cried. "He's our friend. Besides, he belongs to me and . . . and I . . . I . . ."

"You what?" the King asked with a slight smile.

"I love him!" Sarah said, as she looked down at the Emerald Bear.

"Harummmph!" the King said, clearing his throat. "Well, that does complicate things. But the law is the law, and he must be punished."

"What did he do?" Benjamin asked.

"Do!" the King exclaimed. "Why, he is a deserter. He was the Captain of the Bear Guard, and one day I commanded him to go to the Windy Woods and seek out the fairies that live there. Their Queen knows of the Legend and is the keeper of the golden keys of the tunnels to the Outside World.

"The Captain never came back," the King said. "He deserted the Emerald Bears of Ursanor."

The Captain had been listening quietly to the King. Finally, he spoke.

"No, Sire, I didn't desert you," he said. "I found the Queen of the Fairies and spoke to her of the Legend. It was she who showed me how to use the golden keys to open the tunnels to the Outside World."

"What is the Legend?" Sarah asked.

The Emerald Bear smiled at Sarah. "The Legend is why the Emerald Bears were made," he said. "The Legend says that we exist to love and protect children and to have children love us in return.

"Those bears whose hearts are the bravest and fullest of love will be rewarded with a golden key to the Outside World of Children. There, we can be happy forever with children to love. I was sent to see if the Legend was true.

"The Queen of the Fairies is the guardian of the keys, and she gives them only to Emerald Bears who are the most worthy. But the Gruffs stole one of the keys, because they wanted children, too, but not to love—to keep as prisoners."

The Emerald Bear turned to look at the King.

"Sire, I didn't desert you or the bears of this castle. The Fairy Queen told me that one of the keys had been stolen, and she showed me the way the Gruffs had gone."

"I followed their trail to the Outside World, Your Majesty, and arrived in time to stop them from stealing a small boy from his very own room while he slept."

"You did battle with the Gruffs?" the King asked, with a hint of excitement.

"I tried my best, Sire," the Captain replied, "but the Gruffs were many, and I fear that they retreated still holding the golden key."

"But you saved the little boy," Benjamin said.

"Perhaps," said the bear, "but during the battle, my foot became caught and I couldn't return to Ursanor. Even if I could return, I didn't know if the Gruffs would come back again. I believed it was my duty to guard the secret door in the closet."

"There, you see!" Sarah cried. "It wasn't his fault!" She looked pleadingly at King Wuzzlefuzz. "Oh, please, you *must* understand now. He was only trying to protect children!"

"Hmmmm, perhaps I've misjudged you, Captain," the King said. "It seems you've conducted yourself quite bravely. You're an Emerald Bear most worthy of the Legend.

"In light of your explanation, I feel I have no choice but to give you back your old command as Captain of my Bear Guard," the King said with a chuckle.

"Hooray! Hooray!" yelled Sergeant Willow, as he danced in circles around the throne room.

"Quite right, Sir, yes indeedy, quite right!" beamed Lieutenant Pitterpatter.

Everyone in the court was clapping and cheering, but Sarah still had a serious look on her face.

"Why, what's wrong, my child?" the King asked. "Aren't you pleased now?"

"Yes, Sir," Sarah replied, "but I was thinking about Rachael and Annie and the others being held prisoner by those mean Gruffs."

The King looked puzzled. "There are other children in Ursanor?"

"Let me explain, Sire," the Captain said. "When Sarah freed me from the closet, there was no one to guard the secret door. The Gruffs returned and stole Sarah's friends."

"Then we must save them!" the King said.

"These have been troubled times since you've been gone, Captain." He looked at a large map on the wall near his throne.

"The Gruffs in the east keep to themselves and never have a kind word for anyone. The Murkies in the south care nothing for the affairs of Ursanor. They care only about their sparklies.

"The Grizzles in the north are a fierce folk, and I fear war between their people and ours. To the west is the unknown land beyond the Windy Woods. Anyone brave enough to venture there has never returned.

"Yes, these are indeed troubled times, but our duty right now is clear," the King continued. "Captain, take as many of my guards as you need, go to the Dark River, and free those children!"

"Oh, thank you, Sir," Sarah said, throwing her arms around the King and squeezing him close. "You are good and wise, just like my Emerald Bear said."

"Harummph!" said the King. "You'd better hurry now. There's no time to lose."

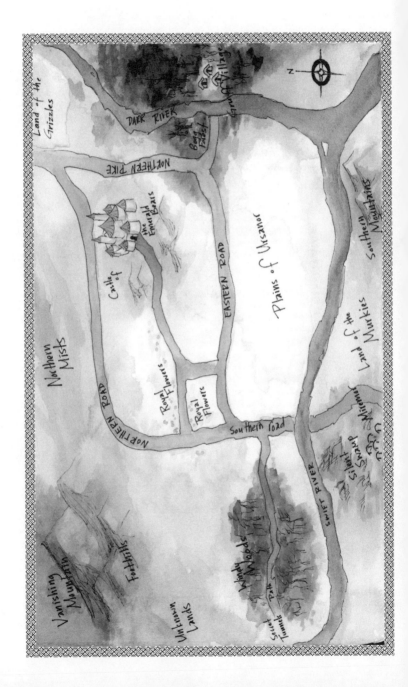

Benjamin and Sarah said good-bye to the King and his court and followed the Emerald Bear, Sergeant Willow, and Lieutenant Pitterpatter out of the throne room.

In the castle courtyard, the Bear Guard gathered quickly, all in their chocolate brown uniforms and with their swords at their sides.

Soon three columns of Emerald Bears stood at the ready, and Sergeant Willow called the guard to attention.

"All present, sir." He saluted Lieutenant Pitterpatter.

"All present, Captain," Pitterpatter said as he saluted the Guard Captain.

The bear smiled at Sarah and Benjamin. "We have all the help we need now!"

"Just one more thing, sir," Sergeant Willow said. "This is for you."

He held up a brand new officer's coat with lots of gold braid and a golden medal on the chest to replace the uniform the Captain lost fighting the Gruffs.

"The King wanted you to be dressed properly to command the Bear Guard."

Sarah's Emerald Bear looked pleased, as he quickly put on the coat, then the hat and sword that came with it.

Sarah felt very proud. She and Benjamin grinned at each other, as they and the Bear Guard made their way out of the castle. They headed for the Dark River, and the home of the Gruffs.

CHAPTER FOUR

The sun was halfway across the sky as the brave group of friends made its way along the road from the castle, past the hills and streams of the King's meadows, and beyond to where the road forked, showing the way to the Dark River.

"I hope Rachael and the others are all right," Sarah said.

"Yes," Benjamin replied. "You know how easily Matt gets scared. The sooner we get there, the better." He looked at the Emerald Bear. "Is it very far?" he asked.

"Just to the other side of Bogg Forest," the bear said, pointing ahead.

Benjamin and Sarah saw that the road ahead entered a very deep and dark wood. None of the trees had any leaves on them, just dark and twisting branches.

"What a horrible place," Sarah said. "It's so creepy."

"Creepy. Creepy, yes indeedy," Lieutenant Pitterpatter said. "It's so dark it makes me sleepy."

"You could sleep anywhere!" Sergeant Willow said.

"We'd all better keep our eyes open," said the Captain of the Bear Guard. "Pass the word to everyone to keep a sharp lookout for any Gruffs!"

They made their way carefully along the winding road that went through the middle of Bogg Forest, with each bear in each column looking all around for any sign of the Gruffs.

Suddenly, the road in the forest split into two roads. One went up and to the left, the other down and to the right.

"Which way, Captain?" Sergeant Willow asked.

"I don't know," he answered. "I've never actually been to the Gruff Village before. I'm not sure anyone has."

"Oh, no!" Sarah cried. "If we go the wrong way, we'll never find our friends."

"Listen!" Benjamin whispered. "Somebody's coming!"

Everyone was very quiet, and from up the road to the left, they heard footsteps and deep, low voices.

"Quickly, everyone off of the road!" commanded the Captain.

The columns of Bear Guards obeyed at once and scattered into the darkness of the forest on both sides of the road. Sarah knelt beside her bear, and Benjamin beside Sergeant Willow.

Down the high road came five strange-looking figures clad in dark robes. They all had hoods surrounding their heads. Each carried a walking stick. As they drew near, Sarah could see big, round noses sticking out of their hoods. Some had long mustaches under their noses, and others had long beards that hung down.

"Gruffs!" whispered her Emerald Bear.

They watched the five Gruffs make their way down the road to the right and disappear into the darkness of the forest.

When the last Gruff was out of sight, Sarah's Emerald Bear jumped back onto the road and circled his arm in the air as a signal for the others to join him.

"We must follow those Gruffs," he said. "Maybe they'll lead us to the Gruff Village."

"Then let's hurry!" Benjamin said.

"Where's Lieutenant Pitterpatter?" asked Sergeant Willow, looking around.

"I thought he was with you," the Captain said.

Everyone looked for the missing bear, but the dark of the forest was too deep. Sarah began to panic. First her friends disappeared, now Lieutenant Pitterpatter was gone. Had the Gruffs captured him?

Then Sergeant Willow heard snoring coming from behind a nearby bush.

Sure enough, the two green feet of the sleeping Lieutenant could be seen sticking out the side of the bush. Sarah breathed a sigh of relief.

The Captain smiled. "Would someone mind waking the Lieutenant and asking him to join us?"

Two of the Bear Guards ran over to the bush and jerked Lieutenant Pitterpatter to his feet. The bear yawned and rubbed his eyes.

"Did you have a nice nap?" asked his captain.

"Yes, sir. Yes indeedy!" Lieutenant Pitterpatter said, his green face turning a little red.

Once again the Bear Guard made its way down the road, staying just behind the Gruffs and out of sight.

The road wound down and around, down and around, until finally, they heard the sound of running water and saw the lights of small cabins up ahead. They had arrived at the Dark River and the Gruff Village.

The Captain stopped the Guard at the edge of the forest, so they could see the village and not be seen themselves.

"Look!" cried Sarah. "In the middle of the village!"

Benjamin and her Emerald Bear looked to where Sarah was pointing.

In the village was a cleared circular area, surrounded by Gruff cabins. In the center of the circle was a large wooden

cage. Inside the cage sat Annie, Rachael, Matt, and the twins, Josh and Jeremy.

Matt's face looked very frightened, but the twins looked mad. They looked like they wanted to get at those Gruffs, but the door of the cage was held fast by thick rope.

There were Gruffs all around the circle, going this way and that way. Near the cage stood a very large Gruff.

Around his dark hood he wore a great golden chain and on that chain was something very special.

"Look—around his neck," the Captain whispered. He pointed at the glittering chain. "The stolen key! He must be the Gruff Leader."

Sarah turned to the bear. "How are we ever going to get them out of there?"

"Don't worry, Sarah," he said. "Do you see that large cabin by the edge of the river? My guess is that is where the Gruffs keep their fish.

"Gruffs love to fish. All day long and all night long, they fish the Dark River and put their catch in the fish cabin.

"My Guard and I will charge that cabin, and the Gruffs will think we're trying to steal their fish. When they come after us, I want five Bear Guards to sneak into the circle and free the children."

"Who will lead the five Bear Guards?" asked Lieutenant Pitterpatter.

"You will," his Captain said. "That is, if you can manage to stay awake along the way."

Lieutenant Pitterpatter saluted sharply. "You can count on me, yes indeedy, you can count on me!"

Benjamin wrinkled his nose. "Why do I feel worried?" he teased.

"Let's do it!" said the Captain of the Bear Guard. He nodded to Sergeant Willow and the bears all drew their swords.

"Just one thing," Sarah said, looking down at the ground. "I don't want anyone to get hurt, even Gruffs."

"It's okay, Sarah," her Emerald Bear said with a smile. "These swords make better whackers than they do stickers."

Then he commanded, "Sergeant Willow, blow the charge!"

"Yes, sir!" said Sergeant Willow, as he turned to the bear bugler. "Corporal Toots, blow the charge!"

The Bear Guard bugler took a deep breath and blew a large bellow on his horn. With a loud yell, the Captain ran from the trees of the forest toward the fish cabin, with Sergeant Willow and the rest of the Bear Guard charging right behind him.

The Gruffs were completely surprised by the noise of the bugle and the charge of the Guard. They started to scatter in all directions, until the Gruff Leader held up his hand.

"They're heading for the fish cabin!" he yelled. "Follow me!"

Soon, all the Gruffs were running for the edge of the river and the fish cabin.

"Now!" said Lieutenant Pitterpatter, as he led the five Bear Guards and Sarah and Benjamin toward the circle in the Gruff Village.

In a few steps, the Lieutenant reached the door of the cage. With one sweep of his sword, he cut the knot on the rope that held the door shut.

"Who are you?" Rachael asked, as the bear stepped inside.

"Lieutenant Pitterpatter, at your service!" he said, with a snappy salute. "I'm here to rescue you."

"Oh, thank you!" Rachael said, hugging the bear with both arms and lifting him off his feet.

"Well, he's not all by himself," Sarah laughed, as she stuck her head in the door of the cage.

"Sarah," the friends all shouted together, "and Benjamin, too!"

The friends embraced each other, shook hands with the Bear Guards, and danced around with delight. But Rachael wouldn't let go of Lieutenant Pitterpatter's arm, and he couldn't stop smiling up at her.

"I thought you didn't like green bears," Benjamin teased.

"Well, I, uh . . . I guess I was wrong. I'm very sorry," she said, looking down at her feet.

"No time for that," Lieutenant Pitterpatter said. "Let's get out of here."

He led the children and Bear Guards out of the cage, across the village circle and in the direction of the river, where the sounds of battle were heard.

As they came closer, they saw that there wasn't a battle going on after all.

When they reached the river, what they saw made them fall on the ground with laughter. It was clear the Gruffs were no match for the Bear Guards.

Every time a Gruff raised his walking stick to swing at a bear, a Bear Guard whacked him on the rump with the flat side of his sword.

"Whack," went the Bear Guards.

"Ouch," said the Gruffs.

"Whack," went the Bear Guards.

"Yeoww," wailed the Gruffs.

Near the fish cabin, Sarah saw her bear and the Gruff Leader standing face to face.

"Stop! We give up!" said the Gruff Leader. "Take our fish if you must, but leave us alone!"

"We don't want your fish," the Captain said sternly. "We only want the children."

The Gruff Leader turned and saw that the children had been set free.

"Then we have lost the treasure we searched so long for," he said sadly. "When we heard of the Legend, it told that the Children of the Outside World possess something more valuable than fish. Something called 'fun.'

"We grow weary of the loneliness and darkness that surrounds us, and have searched all the children's pockets for the treasure the Legend said would make us happy. But we haven't been able to find their games, or songs, or rhymes, or stories, or any of the fun things we know that children possess."

Sarah walked up to the Gruff Leader. Through the darkness of his hood, she saw the sadness in his eyes.

"These are not things you can steal by locking someone in a cage," she said. "These are things you *learn* by playing with others.

"We could teach you the games we know, and the rhymes, and the songs, and the stories, and then you could play for yourselves, any time you want to," she added with a soft smile.

"You would do that—for us?" asked the Gruff Leader.

"Sure," Rachael said, still holding Lieutenant Pitterpatter's arm. "All you had to do was ask us."

All the children laughed. All the Emerald Bears laughed. And slowly, for the first time in their lives, the Gruffs started to laugh.

At first, it was like a giggle, but then it got louder and heartier and spread from Gruff to Gruff, until each and every one was laughing so hard, he had to hold his belly.

Some Gruffs laughed until tears came to their eyes and some laughed until they snorted through their big round noses and some laughed until the hoods from their robes fell back from their heads.

The children saw that each Gruff had a round, bald head with big ears, bushy eyebrows, and eyes that twinkled for the first time.

CHAPTER FIVE

The children spent the rest of the afternoon teaching the Gruffs all the fun things they knew, all of their games and all of their songs and all of their rhymes and all of their stories.

The Gruffs played with the children and the Gruffs played with the bears, and soon, Gruffs were playing with Gruffs.

Sarah was teaching the Gruff Leader how to jump rope when her Emerald Bear approached. He was out of breath from running foot races. "It's time for us to go," he said.

"Thank you, Sarah," the Gruff Leader said. "Thank you all!"

"Just one more thing," said the Captain, pointing to the golden key around the leader's neck.

"Ah, yes," the Gruff Leader said, taking the key off and placing it in the bear's hand. "We won't need to go to the Outside World anymore."

"Thank you," the Captain of the Bear Guard said. "You've all learned something important from these children about how to get along with others.

"Don't let it end here. You'd be welcome as friends in the castle of King Wuzzlefuzz. You must come there for a visit, and soon!"

"We will. I promise!" the Gruff Leader said.

The children waved good-bye and fell in place behind the Bear Guard as they marched back to Bogg Forest.

"I have a feeling that the Emerald Bears and the Gruffs are going to become good friends," Benjamin said to Sarah with a wink.

Soon, the sounds of the Dark River and the lights of the Gruff Village faded, and they hurried quickly through the darkness of the woods and along the roads that wound through Ursanor.

In those last moments of twilight, the trip back seemed much shorter to Benjamin and Sarah than when they began their long journey.

Sarah's bear raised his arm and the long line of bears and children came to a halt.

"We must move quickly now," the bear told the chidren. "I must get you to the Windy Woods before the sun goes down completely. Once the sun sets, you can't return to the Outside World. When it is night in the Outside World, it is day in Ursanor, and when it is night here, it is day in your world.

"Lieutenant Pitterpatter will return to the castle with the Bear Guard, and I will lead you down this road to the Windy Woods."

Rachael looked like she wanted to cry. "Oh, please," she said, "couldn't Lieutenant Pitterpatter come just a little further with us? Please?"

"Very well," the Captain said with a laugh. "Sergeant Willow can lead the guards back."

He turned to Sergeant Willow and said, "Tell His Majesty of all that happened today and inform him that Lieutenant Pitterpatter and I will escort the children safely to the tunnels of the Windy Woods."

"Yes, sir." Sergeant Willow saluted. "It's a pleasure to serve with you again, Captain." The bears exchanged smiles.

The bear sergeant and the guards marched along the road toward the castle. As they passed the children, the seven friends all saluted at the same time.

"Thank you! Thank you!" the children shouted to them.

The Bear Guards held their heads up high, for they were very proud.

Lieutenant Pitterpatter smiled at his Captain. "Quite an adventure, yes indeedy, quite an adventure."

Sarah's bear waved the children on and the small group continued along the winding road, past the King's royal flowers, and on into the Windy Woods.

The bear led them into the very center of the woods, then suddenly turned off from the forest path and walked down to the edge of a small stream. The children followed.

By the edge of the stream was a very, very small house, no higher than Sarah's knees.

"Who lives here?" Annie asked.

"The guardian of the golden keys—The Queen of the Fairies," the bear replied.

As the group neared the tiny home, a strange blue light appeared at the door, lifted into the air, and hung above their heads.

"It's her!" whispered Lieutenant Pitterpatter.

"Welcome to you, Captain," a soft voice from the blue light said. "We of Ursanor have much to thank you for today. You have saved the children of the Outside World from the village of the Gruffs and found the stolen key of the secret tunnels."

"How do you know all this?" Lieutenant Pitterpatter asked shyly.

"I know all that happens in Ursanor," the light replied.

Then the light moved directly over the head of Sarah's Emerald Bear and spoke kindly to him.

"I know your heart is full of brave deeds and also full of love for children. It is for these reasons that I command you to keep this golden key.

"It is your reward, Captain. You belong in the Outside World of Children, for you love them and they love you. You are a most worthy Emerald Bear."

Sarah picked up her bear and hugged him deeply. "Does this mean you can stay with me forever?"

"Yes, Sarah, if you want me," the bear said.

"Oh, I do!" She grinned and kissed him on his nose.

The Fairy Queen said, "Place the golden key against your heart and think of all the love you have for children."

The Emerald Bear did as she commanded and closed his brown eyes tightly. He thought and thought.

Suddenly, the bushes on the other side of the stream began to rustle. They moved slowly at first, and then they jumped apart. There was the tunnel!

The Captain opened his eyes. "I did it!" he called out.

He took Sarah and Benjamin by the hand and led them into the entrance of the tunnel. Annie and Matt came next, then Josh and Jeremy.

Rachael started to follow. "Let's go," she said, smiling at Lieutenant Pitterpatter.

"No, Rachael," the Fairy Queen said. "He can't go with you."

"But why?" Rachael asked, with tears welling up in her eyes.

"Only one Emerald Bear can go through this tunnel. There are many secret doors and tunnels, but each Emerald Bear must find his own, if he proves himself worthy of a key," the Queen replied.

"But Lieutenant Pitterpatter is very brave," Rachael pleaded.

"Perhaps," said the Queen, "but this tunnel isn't for him."

"You'd better hurry, Rachael. There's not much time," Lieutenant Pitterpatter said. "The sun has almost fully set."

"I don't want to leave you," Rachael said sadly.

"I know," said the bear, "but if you don't go now, you won't ever get home."

Rachael looked at the edge of the sun, settling behind the trees of the Windy Woods.

"I won't ever forget you," she said, as she turned toward the tunnel entrance.

Just inside, she turned and called back, "I love you!"

As she spoke these words, the light around the Fairy Queen grew brighter.

"I love you, too!" Lieutenant Pitterpatter answered. Then the tunnel closed behind Rachael.

The bear stood alone with the Fairy Queen. He couldn't tell where the tunnel entrance had been.

"It seems your heart is not only brave, but also full of love for children," the Queen said.

"I can't tell anymore," the bear said sadly. "All I know is that it hurts right here." He pointed to his chest. "Yes indeedy, right here." He stood for a moment, then sighed, "I'd better start back for the castle."

As he turned to go, the Queen of the Fairies kissed him on his brown nose and slipped something around his neck.

It was very shiny and it was made of gold.

Back in the tunnel, the children kept close behind the Emerald Bear as he led them to the far end and to the small green door.

They scrambled through the door and were once again in Sarah's bedroom closet.

They opened the closet door, walked through the bedroom and into the hallway, then tiptoed past Benjamin's room. Sarah noticed that the room was exactly as she and Benjamin had left it.

Annie and Matt ran ahead calling, "Mommy! Daddy! We're back! We're back!"

The other children quickly followed.

Sarah stopped at the top of the stairs with her Emerald Bear. *Where's Rachael?* she thought, and as she turned to look, Rachael stepped through the bedroom door.

"Where were you?" Sarah asked.

"I had to say good-bye to someone," Rachael said sadly.

Sarah put her arm around her friend and held her close. "I understand," she said. "Maybe my Emerald Bear can help."

"Can you?" Sarah asked, as she turned to look at the bear.

Her Emerald Bear did not answer.

"What's wrong? Can't you hear me?" Sarah asked.

Still the bear did not answer. He leaned against the wall by the staircase and stared straight ahead.

Just then, Mr. Williams bounded up the stairs. "Sarah! And Rachael, too! We were worried when you weren't with the others."

"We're coming, Daddy," Sarah said, as she and Rachael turned to follow their friends down to the big living room. Sarah clutched her bear close to her.

The other children were already in their parents' arms, chatting away very excitedly.

"Wait a minute! One at a time!" the twins' mother said. "We've been looking everywhere for you, and now you all come out of the upstairs bedroom. I don't understand."

Sheriff Parker was there, too. "Yes, where did you youngsters go off to, anyway?" he asked.

The children all started to jabber once again. The parents heard words like tunnel, castle, bears, Gruffs, and fairies.

"Hold it! Hold it!" Sheriff Parker said at last. "I don't think we're going to get to the bottom of this tonight. The important thing is that you are all safe and sound.

"Why don't you kids go to bed, and we'll straighten this out in the morning. Gruffs, indeed! You youngsters have some imagination!"

The Sheriff said Good night and walked out with Josh and Jeremy's parents, who carried the twins to their car. Annie and Matt followed with their parents.

As Rachael left with her mother and father, she hugged Benjamin and Sarah and then looked at the Emerald Bear still snuggled in Sarah's arms.

"Thanks, Captain," Rachael said. "You really are somebody special, after all."

The bear stared back in silence, but the look on his furry face seemed to say that everything was going to be all right.

After everyone had left, Mr. and Mrs. Williams took their children back upstairs to tuck them into their sleeping bags again.

As Mr. Williams was helping Sarah into her bag, he said, "You two don't usually make up stories. I have a feeling more happened than you're telling us."

"You probably wouldn't believe us anyway," Benjamin said, as he took off his baseball cap. "I'm not sure we believe it ourselves."

Mr. Williams looked down at the Emerald Bear, who was sitting on the floor at the foot of Sarah's bag. He bent down and picked the bear up.

"This bear didn't have a coat and hat before. Where did you find them, Sarah? And where did you get this little sword? It almost looks real."

Sarah pretended to be falling asleep and mumbled something Mr. Williams did not understand. Then he noticed the chain around the bear's neck.

"You know," he said to Mrs. Williams, "if I didn't know better, I'd say the key around this bear's neck was made of real gold."

"I think you need some sleep, too," Mrs. Williams laughed.

Mr. Williams placed the bear on the floor beside Sarah.

"Strange. It's all very strange."

They kissed their children Good night and tiptoed out.

"Sarah," Benjamin said, as he drifted off to sleep, "do you think it all really happened?"

Sarah looked at her Emerald Bear, who gave her a big wink.

"Of course it did, silly!" Sarah and the bear said at the same time.

The ride home was a long one for Rachael.

Even as her parents were placing her in her own bed, she couldn't help but think about all that had happened.

Her mother turned a night-light on for her, kissed her, and then left the room.

Rachael tried to drop off to sleep, but it wasn't easy. She kept seeing the adventure in her head, and hearing it, too.

In fact, even now she thought she heard footsteps, tiny footsteps.

No, it couldn't be footsteps; she must be dreaming.

But, yes, it was footsteps! They were coming from the closet. Rachael decided to be brave, like her faraway friend Lieutenant Pitterpatter was brave.

She peeked over the covers at the closet door. It slowly began to open and a somewhat familiar and chubby head peeked around the corner of the door.

"Very long tunnel, yes indeedy, very long tunnel," the bear said. "I thought I was never going to find the end. Almost couldn't squeeze through the door, too!"

"Lieutenant Pitterpatter! It's you!" Rachael squealed, as she jumped out of bed. She was at the closet in two leaps and scooped the bear off his feet.

"You're here! You're here!" she said, hugging him with all her might.

"Yes," the bear grunted, "but I'll be here, there, and everywhere if you hug me any harder!"

They both laughed.

Rachael carried Lieutenant Pitterpatter over to her bed and placed him gently on the pillow beside her.

She smiled at him as they snuggled under the covers. Soon she felt a warm sleep creeping over her. As she closed her eyes, she thought, *I have someone special to guard me tonight. I have my very own Emerald Bear.*

ABOUT THE AUTHOR

Ken Orchard pilots an EMS helicopter and practices medicine in Nashville, Tennessee. The Chicago native penned *The Emerald Bear* after his daughter, Jamie, requested that he write her a story. *The Emerald Bear* is his first work about the mysterious land of Ursanor.

ABOUT THE ILLUSTRATOR

In addition to being an illustrator, Jenny L. Kilgore is also a park ranger for the state of Tennessee. Born in Gatlinburg, Tennessee, she graduated from East Tennessee State University with bachelor's and master's degrees in history. She resides in northeast Tennessee with her husband, David, and several furry friends.

Join Sarah and her friends as they travel back to Ursanor to help King Wuzzlefuzz find the Lost Royal Amulet.